I Want to be a Writer

PRAISE FOR *STORYSHARES*

"One of the brightest innovators and game-changers in the education industry."
– Forbes

"Your success in applying research-validated practices to promote literacy serves as a valuable model for other organizations seeking to create evidence-based literacy programs."
- Library of Congress

"We need powerful social and educational innovation, and Storyshares is breaking new ground. The organization addresses critical problems facing our students and teachers. I am excited about the strategies it brings to the collective work of making sure every student has an equal chance in life."
– Teach For America

"Around the world, this is one of the up-and-coming trailblazers changing the landscape of literacy and education."
- International Literacy Association

"It's the perfect idea. There's really nothing like this. I mean wow, this will be a wonderful experience for young people."   - Andrea Davis Pinkney, Executive Director, Scholastic

"Reading for meaning opens opportunities for a lifetime of learning. Providing emerging readers with engaging texts that are designed to offer both challenges and support for each individual will improve their lives for years to come. Storyshares is a wonderful start."
- David Rose, Co-founder of CAST & UDL

I Want to be a Writer

Anya Ivan

STORYSHARES

Story Share, Inc.
New York. Boston. Philadelphia

Copyright © 2022 Anya Ivan

All rights reserved.

Published in the United States by Story Share, Inc.

The characters and events in this book are fictitious. Any similarity to real persons, living or dead, is entirely coincidental.

Storyshares
Story Share, Inc.
24 N. Bryn Mawr Avenue #340
Bryn Mawr, PA 19010-3304
www.storyshares.org

Inspiring reading with a new kind of book.

Interest Level: Middle School
Grade Level Equivalent: 3.7

9781642614671

Book design by Storyshares

Printed in the United States of America

Storyshares Presents

1

My name is Alex Ponte and I want to be a writer.

I have wanted to be a writer for a whole year now. But I have two problems: 1.) I am twelve and 2.) I do not understand English grammar.

When I decided to be a writer, I looked on the back of all my mom's books. She has fifty-four books. Twenty-seven have the picture of the author on the back cover. All writers are old.

My mom says I think everyone over the age of twelve is old. I do not think that is true. My sister is sixteen and I do not think she is old.

My sister says I am stupid. She thinks my idea of being a writer is stupid.

I am not very worried about what my sister says. She thinks the entire world is stupid. She discovered the word "stupid" a couple of years ago when we moved to Canada. Today, she used it seven times during breakfast and fifteen times during dinner. I know because I counted.

* * *

We moved to Canada two years ago. Only my mom, my sister, and I moved here. My father stayed in the "old country." He left us long before we moved.

My mom said he left us because babies interfered with his writing. She told that to one of her new friends here in Canada. That is how I found out my father is a writer.

I did not know what the word "interfered" meant. My mother said it like it was a bad word. I did not want to ask my sister what it meant. I did not want to hear the word "stupid" again.

* * *

Last year, I wrote my first story.

I was very proud of it. It was a story with birds, dogs, ponies, dragons, and cats. I also added a talking snake for good measure.

I think it was the talking snake that ruined the story.

Mrs. Skoll, my English teacher, gave me an insufficient. She said my grammar was atrocious. It sounded really bad, so I looked up that word in the dictionary. It meant "really bad." Go figure.

When she gave me the paper back, I asked her if she liked the story.

"I will like a story that I can read," she said.

For a couple of days after that, I was sad.

2

My mom had to take the driver test. She is a good driver, and she has never had an accident.

She failed the test.

I was there. When the driver instructor gave her the paper, my mother thanked him very politely.

We went home by bus, in silence. At home, I asked my mom if she was mad at the instructor for failing her.

"Why would I be mad?" she asked. "He is there to make sure that people who drive know what they are doing."

"But you are a good driver!"

"I will learn to be a better driver and next time I will pass the test."

She failed two more times. In the end, she passed the test. We had ice cream to celebrate. I asked her if she was happy.

"I am happy I passed the test." She gave me our secret wink. "I am happier that I can keep you safer now."

* * *

My mom is a good driver. After studying for her exam, she is even better. Even if I got an insufficient grade on my story, it does not mean I am a bad writer. It just means I can be better.

This past summer, I asked everybody to teach me grammar, except for my sister. I don't think she even knows that grammar exists. She just writes texts on her iPhone with lots of hearts and exclamation marks.

My mom tried to help me. She took my textbooks and learned at night. She showed me what she learned the next day. I was more confused.

In the end, my mom asked our neighbor's daughter, Amanda, to help me. My mom cleaned their house for four hours on Saturdays.

Amanda taught me grammar twice a week. Amanda was a beautiful girl. I spent the first two weeks blushing and stammering. I had no idea what she was teaching me.

My mom asked if I found the lessons helpful. I did not want to disappoint her. I told her I learned a lot.

"He is in love with Amanda," my sister said. "I bet he does not remember anything he learned. He is that stupid."

My mom told my sister to stop calling me names. After that, she turned to me.

"I don't think you should let your interest in Amanda interfere with your learning."

This is how I found out that "interfere" was not a bad word. I promised my mom that I would try to focus more.

The next time I went for a lesson with Amanda, I focused on what I did not like about her. She talked too loudly, and she always had food around her mouth. I don't like people that don't wipe their mouths.

I stopped blushing and stammering, and I started learning. By the end of the summer, I knew all the parts of a sentence. I started to understand verbs. I even practiced spelling on my own with a spelling bee app.

I was getting closer to becoming a writer.

3

We moved to this neighborhood because my sister skipped school to be with a boy. My mom decided it was time for us to move to a better place.

My mom said my sister will skip school again for a boy. She hopes that next time the boy will not be a criminal. She told that to her friend. I heard it by accident, when my ear was stuck to the vent that went from the basement to the living room.

I do not mind that we moved. I got to move all my books. I don't have many real friends, but I have many imaginary friends from my books. I can read for hours. I have books I have read a hundred times. I like sitting there and imagining my heroes' great adventures.

*** * * ***

I started at a new school in September. That is how I met Mr. Owen. He is my new English teacher.

On the first week, Mr. Owen asked us to write a story.

I was confident this time, but I left out the talking snake. Even though I knew better grammar, I really wanted to impress Mr. Owen.

The next week, he brought back our stories. He was not impressed. He also gave me an *insufficient*.

I was very sad. For the rest of the class, I struggled to hide my tears.

I will never be a writer.

*** * * ***

Mr. Owen stopped me after class.

"I see my grade made you very upset. I am sorry. I think you have great potential and by the end of the year I am certain you will improve your grade."

"I want to be a writer" I said.

"That is a very impressive goal for your life."

"No, you don't understand. I don't want to be a writer when I am old. I want to be a writer now."

Mr. Owen took my paper and looked at it again.

"I gave you an insufficient because I had a hard time following your story. I think I know what the problem is."

I tried not to look at him. I did not want him to know how much I wanted his help.

"I think you should start writing about things you know. You should start keeping a journal."

Just like that, I lost my hope.

"I don't want to keep a journal like a girl."

Mr. Owen nodded. "I understand," he told me. "But most great writers kept journals. Some of them were later published."

He went to a bookshelf and took out a book. "This is a journal kept by a very famous writer when he was a little older than you."

He gave me the book. He told me to come back in a couple of weeks and talk to him about it.

4

I made a journal from an old notepad mom brought home from work. I wrote every day before bed. After two weeks, I had almost ten pages that looked the same.

I had breakfast.

I went to school.

I ate lunch in the cafeteria.

I went back to class.

I came home.

I read.

I did my homework.

I took a bath.

I went to bed.

The last sentence was not really true because I wrote it while I was still awake.

* * *

I took my journal pages to Mr. Owen.

"I think people that write journals have a more interesting life. My life is so boring."

He took the notebook and looked through it.

"I don't think they have a more interesting life," he said. "A writer can make the most normal events into extraordinary adventures."

He asked me to put more details in my journal: What time did I have breakfast? Was I alone? How was the weather? What did I have for breakfast?

"That one is simple," I rushed to say. "I always eat Cheerios with cold milk."

Mr. Owen continued: How did the Cheerios taste? What sound did they make when you chewed? What color was the milk when you added Cheerios?

"The next time I read your journal, I want to feel like I am having breakfast with you. I want to be so impressed by your description of the Cheerios that I can never have breakfast cereal again without thinking of what you wrote."

5

The Cheerios Journal Entry

It is seven in the morning and my mom is rushing to get to work. I sit at the table next to the kitchen, eating my bowl of cereal with cold milk.

My mom drinks coffee every morning. One cup before she leaves the house. I start eating when she starts brewing the coffee.

She is brewing the coffee on the stove, like in the old country. Someone gave us a coffee machine, but she only uses it for guests. She says the coffee does not taste the same.

The smell of coffee grows stronger with every bite I take.

When I start eating, the Cheerios are crunchy and sweet. They make a popping sound in my mouth, like when you bounce a ball on the asphalt. They get soggier with every spoonful.

At the end of my bowl, the Cheerios taste slightly bitter. I think the smell of the coffee mixes with the taste of my food and changes it. I like Cheerios so much that I usually pour a second bowl.

This morning, my sister took the last drop of milk before I could pour another bowl. I told my mother. She sighed and said that she will have to stop at the grocery store on her way home. I know she is tired from work. I told her I could meet her at the bus stop and help her carry the groceries.

She kissed the top of my head and thanked me.

My sister said this was stupid.

* * *

I followed Mr. Owen's advice. I wrote about everything that I noticed in a day. Sometimes, I would write about school. Sometimes, about breakfast. My journal entries got longer and longer.

With every page, writing about stuff got easier. Mr. Owen's classes helped a lot. We talked about plots and characters. We read books with a critical eye instead of just for entertainment. My grades started getting better.

My head was bursting with stories. I tried again to write about dragons. What I could clearly see in my head never made it onto paper the same way.

I saw majestic mountains. When I tried to describe them, they sounded more like the hills in the old country.

I saw epic fights with monsters and dragons. My descriptions sounded more like the neighbor's dog fighting with a stray cat.

I tried to read some of my mom's books to find inspiration. They were boring. For many pages they just talked about feelings.

I Want to be a Writer

6

My sister had been gone for two weeks when I decided I would not let her departure interfere with my writing.

I sat at my desk for two hours, trying to string words together.

"Write about what you know." That is what Mr. Owen always said.

I am twelve years old, I wrote. *I have lived on two continents. I have moved twelve times since I can remember. We moved five times in the old country and seven times since we arrived in Canada.*

All the places were different. I started describing each of them. I realized that I didn't remember a lot about some of the places we lived.

I forgot all my friends from the old country. I never really made new friends here.

I destroyed the pages I wrote and I started over.

I was going to write about what I knew. The only person I truly knew was my mom.

* * *

My sister came back a week later.

Her presence interfered with her boyfriend's ability to date other girls. He was not happy and he sent her away.

My sister and my mom talked and cried for a whole evening. I stayed away. I was busy writing my story.

I took my story to Mr. Owen. He told me it was good. He told me to go home and write the story again. I was confused. I thought I already did that.

Mr. Owen explained that I wrote the first draft. Now, I had to go home and write it again.

I was still confused until I started writing. The second time, my ideas were crystal clear in my head. Words came to me so easily. I wrote the second draft much faster than the first.

I took the story to Mr. Owen again. He asked me to get my mom's approval to get it published. He told me he would help me make the last edits.

I Want to be a Writer

7

My story got published in a literary journal for children my age. I even have my picture in it and a little biography.

I told Mr. Owen I was a writer now. He looked at me, surprised.

"Alex, you were always a writer. From the first time you sat down and wrote a story, you could call yourself a writer. Now, you are a published writer."

He gave me two copies of the journal to take home to my mom.

I ran all the way home with my two copies of the journal.

It was funny I ran because it wasn't necessary. My mom was not home and she would not be for another hour.

I did not want my sister to be the first to read my story.

I waited for my mom at the door. Before she could take off her shoes, I pushed the journal in front of her eyes.

She sighed.

"Just like your father…" She sounded so sad.

* * *

In the old country, we have a large family. My mother has four sisters. They are all married. They all have children. Their husbands have brothers and sisters. My grandparents have brothers and sisters.

Most of my family lives in the same city, so they visit each other often. The kids are taken care of by the family.

I was one year old when my father left us. He moved to the capital for more opportunities.

When we used to gather for birthdays or other celebrations, my family spoke of two things: how my father was good-for-nothing and how much I looked like my father.

One day, I asked my mom if our family hated me. She asked me why I would think that.

"I look like my father," I said. "They hate my father."

My mom hugged me tight. That night, she got on the phone and told the entire family to shut up. They did, but I could still feel their looks.

✷ ✷ ✷

When we moved to Canada, my father was too busy to come and take us to the airport. At that time, I had not seen him in four years. Now, it would be six.

My mom never talks badly about my father. She always told me he loves me very much and he wishes he could be with us. I know it is not true. I never told my mom that.

I know people have a mom and a dad and they do things together as a family. I have never known what it's like to have a dad, so I don't really miss it. I don't miss him. I don't care what he does. If he is too busy to call, why should I care?

There were two instances when my mom told me I was like him.

The first time, I spent a day arranging my books in alphabetical order by author. I left the rest of my room a complete disaster.

The second time, I gave her the journal that published my first story.

***

I knew my mom had read the entire story when she came in my room at two in the morning. She woke me up and cried with me in her arms for a long time.

I wrote the story about her. How she goes to work every day, even if she is sick.

How she woke up at three in the morning to make my Halloween costume.

How I never heard her say a bad word about anyone, even if some people were not very nice to her.

She left a good job behind to come to a new country and work hard. For us. To have a better future together.

She left her family behind. She spends every Saturday talking with them, but it is not the same. With every year that passes, they feel further and further away.

My mom would do anything for us. When we did not have money for a tutor, she cleaned houses to help me with my education.

She knows what foods I like and she makes them, even if she does not like them.

When my sister ran from home, she was so worried.

When my sister came back home, she received her with open arms. She is my sister's rock. She is our rock.

8

Here is an excerpt from my story.

My name is Alex Ponte and I want to be a writer, even if I am only twelve years old.

I started to write because my father was a writer.

I continue to write because I have stories in my head that scream to be put on paper.

I will stop writing if it interferes with my family.

I want to be brave like my mother. Just like her, I want to have the courage to always be there for the people who are important to me.

About The Author

Anya Ivan is a new writer from Edmonton, Canada. She is inspired by people's courage in the face of adversity. She hopes her stories will help every person find the hero in themselves.

I Want to be a Writer

About The Publisher

Story Shares is a nonprofit focused on supporting the millions of teens and adults who struggle with reading by creating a new shelf in the library specifically for them. The ever-growing collection features content that is compelling and culturally relevant for teens and adults, yet still readable at a range of lower reading levels.

Story Shares generates content by engaging deeply with writers, bringing together a community to create this new kind of book. With more intriguing and approachable stories to choose from, the teens and adults who have fallen behind are improving their skills and beginning to discover the joy of reading. For more information, visit storyshares.org.

Easy to Read. Hard to Put Down.

Made in the USA
Middletown, DE
20 January 2023

22532613R00026